Izzy the Lizzy

by Renee Riva

illustrated by Steve Björkman

WaterBrook
PRESS

Izzy the Lizzy
Published by WaterBrook Press
2375 Telstar Drive, Suite 160
Colorado Springs, Colorado 80920
A division of Random House, Inc.

Scripture taken from the *Holy Bible, New International Version*®. NIV®. Copyright © 1973, 1978, 1984 by International Bible Society. Used by permission of Zondervan Publishing House. All rights reserved.

ISBN 1-4000-7059-7

Text copyright © 2005 by Renee Riva

Illustrations copyright © 2005 by Steve Björkman

Library of Congress Cataloging-in-Publication Data
Riva, Renee.
    Izzy the lizzy / by Renee Riva ; illustrated by Steve Björkman.— 1st ed.
        p. cm.
    Summary: A hungry lizard's lunch plans change when she makes the acquaintance of a predatory spider and a wise bee.
    ISBN 1-4000-7059-7
    [1. Lizards—Fiction. 2. Spiders—Fiction. 3. Bees—Fiction. 4. Kindness—Fiction. 5. Friendship—Fiction. 6. Stories in rhyme.] I.
    PZ8.3.R523Iz 2005
    [E]—dc22
                                                          2004027711

Printed in Mexico
2005—First Edition

10 9 8 7 6 5 4 3 2 1

For my Lord Jesus, the Author of mercy

And for Gary~

Mon raison de être

ce côté du ciel.

Thank you for being true.

Love, Boo

Be merciful, just as your Father is merciful.

LUKE 6:36

On the shores of Bitty Bayou,
along a bitsy bog,
a lonely little lizard
lived in a lumpy log.

Outside the lumpy log,
there was a crooked crack.
And when you peeked inside,
two itsy eyes peeked back.

For there lived Izzy Lizzy,
who liked her cozy home,
though sometimes cabin fever
gave her an urge to roam.

One rather rainy morning,
she stepped out in the fog
to spend the day exploring
the beauty of the bog.

As she came upon a clearing,
little Izzy sighed,
for the beauty of the marshes
touched her deep inside.

Through the crags and crannies
she took some time to wander.
Beside a pond of lilies,
Izzy stopped to ponder.

There upon a twisted twig she spied a ditty dot,
which really was a spider no bigger than a jot.

And strung between two branches, she saw a wimpy web.
Smack-dab in the middle was a bitty bee named Jeb.

The way the spider eyed him
gave Izzy just a hunch
the itty bitty Jeb bee
would be the spider's lunch.

Izzy thought to eat the spider,
but she didn't feel
that such a teeny critter
would make much of a meal.

Better yet to wait until
the spider's lunch was done.
Then she'd have the pleasure,
of getting two in one.

Surprised by Izzy's shadow,
the spider got the notion
she would be the lizard's treat
if she made one wrong motion.

Then Izzy asked the spider,
"My dear, what is your name?"
She answered, "Anastasia.
My mother's was the same...

until a lizard ate her
when I was only three.
May I beg your mercy
while I eat this bitty bee?"

Izzy eyed the spider,
who then eyed poor little Jeb,
as he spoke up with courage
while trembling in her web.

"Seems strange you ask for mercy,
yet mercy you withhold
from me, your helpless victim.
That does seem rather cold."

"When someone is shown mercy, shouldn't it be granted by the one who's been set free?" The spider looked enchanted.

"I see your point," the spider said.
"It takes me by surprise.
You possess great wisdom
for a bitty bee your size."

"Bravo!" cried Izzy Lizzy,
amazed by little Jeb.
"May I suggest a picnic
in the fruit orchard instead?"

So the spider granted mercy
unto the bitty bee.
She tore away the tangled web
and set small Jeb bee free.

And Izzy granted mercy
unto the kindly spider.
The three then shared a hearty feast
of apple cakes and cider.

Now on the *Bitty Bayou*,
along a bitsy bog,
upon a tiny twig
that adorns a lumpy log,

there lives a kindly spider,
whose spinning keeps her busy,

beside a bitty beehive,
near best friends, Jeb and Izzy.